# CARS

by Anne Rockwell

E. P. Dutton • New York

Copyright © 1984 by Anne Rockwell
All rights reserved.
Published in the United States by E.P. Dutton, Inc.,
2 Park Avenue, New York, N.Y. 10016
Published simultaneously in Canada by
Fitzhenry & Whiteside Limited, Toronto
Editor: Ann Durell   Designer: Isabel Warren-Lynch
Printed in Hong Kong by South China Printing Co.
First Edition   COBE   10 9 8 7 6 5 4 3 2 1

Library of Congress Cataloging in Publication Data
Rockwell, Anne F.
    Cars.
    Summary: A simple look at cars and their uses.
    1. Automobiles—Juvenile literature.   [1. Automobiles]
I. Title.
TL147.R57   1984   629.2'222   83-14080
ISBN 0-525-44079-8

Cars go everywhere.

They go on six-lane turnpikes

and on dusty, country roads.

They go through dark tunnels

and over airy bridges.

They go fast.

They go slow.

Gasoline makes them go.

There are big cars

and small cars,

old cars

and new cars.

Cars take us far away

and down the street to the store.

Our car is red and shiny.

We get in our car,

and away we go!